GOLLY'S FOLLY

GOLLY'S FOLLY: THE PRINCE WHO WANTED IT ALL

Published by Patrol Books

patrolbooks.com

info@patrolbooks.com

LCCN: 2016946889

ISBN-10: 0-692-69193-6

ISBN-13: 978-0-692-69193-9

Cover Design: Eleazar Ruiz

Lettering: Nathan Yoder

Cover Illustration: Rommel Ruiz

Editor: Rosanne Cornbrooks Catalano

Printed in the United States of America

First Edition 2016

Golly's Folly

THE PRINCE WHO WANTED IT ALL

Written by ELEAZAR & REBEKAH RUIZ

Illustrated by ROMMEL RUIZ

PATROL BOOKS

Acknowledgments

We are overwhelmed by the support of the following individuals:

Nathan Yoder

Courtney Cherest

Titus Richard

Ronald Rabideau

Rene Garzona

Joshua Hill

Thomas Terry

Rosanne Catalano

Justin Dean

Stephen Silver

Matthew Bates

Alan Quinonez

We couldn't have done it without you!

Eleazar & Rebekah Ruiz

For our future kids, we love you and can't wait to meet you!
May you always find satisfaction in things unseen.

Rommel Ruiz

For my wife Anny, and my two daughters Bel and Lyz,
my God-given treasures on earth, I love you.

Once, in a kingdom in a faraway land,
King Zhor made his home in a palace so grand.
He loved his son, Golly, with all of his heart,
But Golly couldn't wait for his own life to start.

King Zhor appeared and Golly saw people bow.

Golly wanted that, too—he wanted it now.

As king, he'd have so many choices to make!

And, thinking just of himself, he made a mistake.

wait for the crown? Grow old, then become king?
No, Golly knew what he wanted more than anything.
"If you step down now, Father, I swear
I will rule wisely over the land in our care."

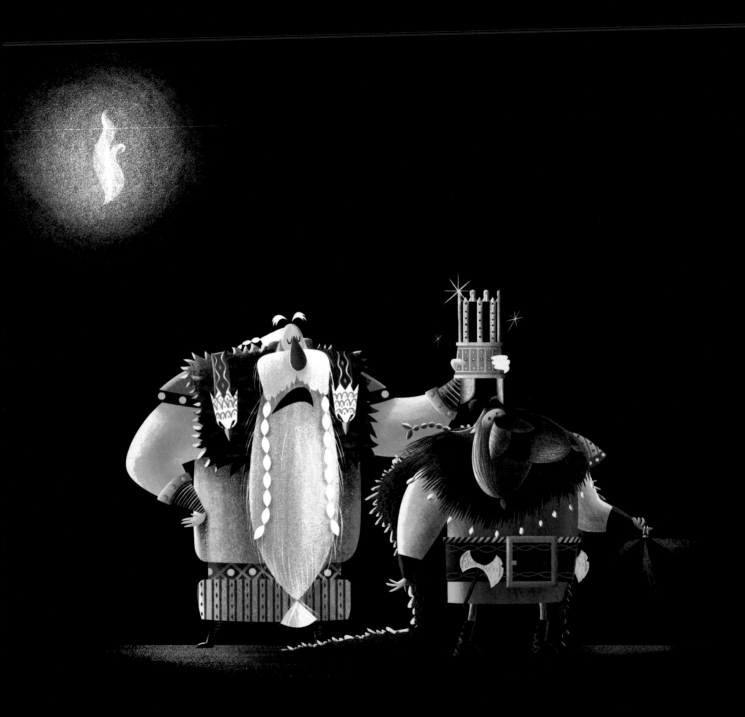

Zhor handed his robe to his eager young son,

Then gave him his crown; the exchange was done.

Now Golly felt happy; his title had a nice ring,

So he showed off a bit on his first day as king.

All the people bowed and admired his clothes,
He smiled in the sun, striking a pose.
He let the light reflect on his shiny gold crown.
His dreams had come true; everyone knew it in town.

He enjoyed the attention, the dancing and fun,
And he liked giving orders to everyone!
He counted his riches, all his gold in a heap,
But after a few months, he still could not sleep.

He sent for Greger, humble and wise,
Who always stood ready to assist and advise.
Greger served his father through thick and thin;
He would bring whatever Golly wanted to him.

Greger came in and bowed, rising to say,
"My king, how may I serve you today?"

"I know what I want—I want to have it all!
I need more possessions at my beck and call!"

"I want flocks of animals and a farm on a hill.
Get some of all kinds—what a thrill!
Build lots of houses, find rings for my hand.
Oh—and I'd like my very own band."

"Oh, King Golly, do not worry.
Whatever you want, I will do in a hurry!"

Soon King Golly had all that he asked for,
But all those things left him looking for more.

He called Greger and asked, "What's the point of this stuff?
I'm still not happy; I've had enough."

"I know what I want—I want to know it all!
Greger! Build a library a hundred feet tall
With shelves full of books all waiting for me
So I can learn everything from A to Z."

"Oh, King Golly, do not worry.
Whatever you want, I will do in a hurry!"

Golly's library was not just for show;
He learned all the things he could possibly know.
He studied all night, then woke up at five;
Everyone called him the Smartest Man Alive.

This brought him happiness for just a few days;
After that, he called Greger, who seemed amazed.

Greger asked, "And how may I serve you today?"

"I know what I want—I want to enjoy it all!
On my birthday, on the twelfth of May,
I want the biggest party ever for my day."

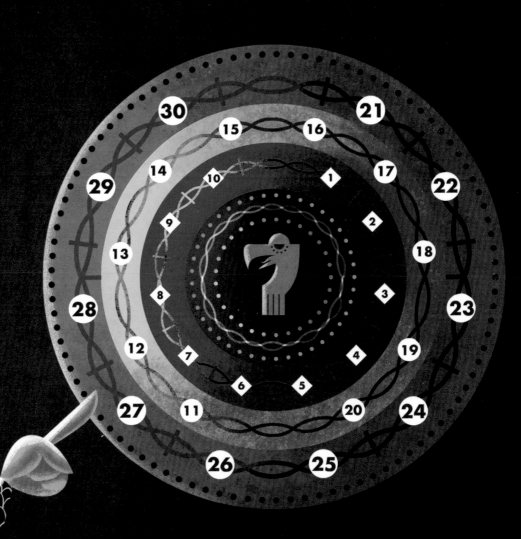

"Oh, King Golly, do not worry.
Whatever you want, I will do in a hurry!"

Of course, Greger jumped straight to his task,

He drew up a plan and he did it fast.

He invited a thousand famous guests,

Who arrived from the North, South, East, and West.

Next on the list, Greger ordered an ice cream-filled cake,
And a feast of the best foods the chef could make.
The guests arrived, laughing, happy, and hearty.
Golly ate and laughed, too, enjoying the party.

Golly ate one piece of cake, then two, three, four!
He stuffed himself till he couldn't eat more.

All through the night, as his tower of gifts grew,

Golly felt strange. What should he do?

He felt sicker and sicker; he could only crawl.

He crept up to his room, then began to bawl.

He felt so alone despite the party crowd.
"I have hundreds of gifts," he cried aloud,
"But no one to share with, no one who cares!"
"What was I thinking?" he asked in despair.

King Zhor came in and helped his son up;
He handed Golly cool water in his own cup.
Golly gazed in wonder at his father's eyes–
Had he always been so loving and wise?

Remembering, Golly looked back on his past.

His father always helped him, whenever he asked.

Whether he thought about his father or not,

King Zhor thought about him and loved him a lot.

When it came to the crown, he'd gladly wait.
The stuff, the facts, the fun might feel great,
But the love of his father made him happy inside
And he had lessons to learn at his father's side.

He had learned King Zhor never let him down,
So, wisely, Golly gave back his father's crown.

He would never be happy with things he could store,
For the love of his father meant so much more.

About the Contributors

Eleazar Ruiz
Author

Eleazar is a graphic designer and illustrator with seven years of experience working simultaneously in the worlds of freelance, in-house teams & design firms. In his professional career he has done anything from leading design teams to being the only in-house designer. That includes art directing for a group of 14 churches with an online audience of millions, a publishing company, and a record label.

In addition to creative arts, Eleazar has deep interest in theology so in 2010 he attended Bible College to pursue a Bachelors in Theological Studies.

eleazarruiz.com

Rebekah Ruiz
Author

Bekah studied Elementary Education at George Fox University in Newberg, Oregon. She spent half of her life in Dallas, Texas and half in Portland, Oregon and has spent her career in various academic settings such as elementary schools, colleges and a library.

She loves the sun, all things silly and teaching a bright-eyed learner! Bekah's ideal Saturday would involve a lot of coffee and friends.

Eleazar and his wife Bekah met at Bible College in 2010. He and Bekah currently reside in greater Seattle, Washington.

Rommel Ruiz
Illustrator

Rommel Ruiz is a designer & illustrator living and working in Los Angeles, CA. Born and raised in the Dominican Republic, Rommel strives to create work that portrays joy, imagination and curiosity. He is always driven by telling a memorable story and crafting powerful messages for clients and audiences.

With over 13 years of experience working as an in-house and freelance designer/illustrator for a variety of industries, Rommel brings diverse talents and artistic perspectives to every project.

He is a happy husband to Anny (also a designer) and a thankful father of two joyful girls.

rommelruiz.com